Careful With That Ball, Eugene!

written and illustrated by

Tohby Riddle

3

ORCHARD BOOKS   NEW YORK

Orchard Books, A division of Franklin Watts, Inc.
387 Park Avenue South, New York, NY 10016

Manufactured in the United States of America. Printed by General Offset Company,
Inc. Bound by Horowitz/Rae. Book design by Mina Greenstein. The text of this
book is set in 22 pt. Melior. The illustrations are watercolor and pen-and-ink.
2 4 6 8 10 9 7 5 3 1

Library of Congress Cataloging-in-Publication Data
Riddle, Tohby.   Careful with that ball, Eugene! / written and illustrated by Tohby
Riddle. 1st American ed. p. cm.
Summary: Depicts all the terrible things that might have happened when Eugene
kicked the ball—but didn't, thanks to his dog.
ISBN 0-531-05917-0   ISBN 0-531-08517-1 (lib. bdg.)
[1. Imagination—Fiction.] I. Title. PZ7.R4168Car 1991 [E]—dc20 90-43015

When Eugene kicked the ball hard . . .

. . . it could have gone through
the McBeavers' front window,

startling Mr. McBeaver,

and right
past the cuckoo clock,

to the table
where the priceless
antique Chinese vase . . .

. . . was.

It could have gone across the dining room,

through the dining room wall,

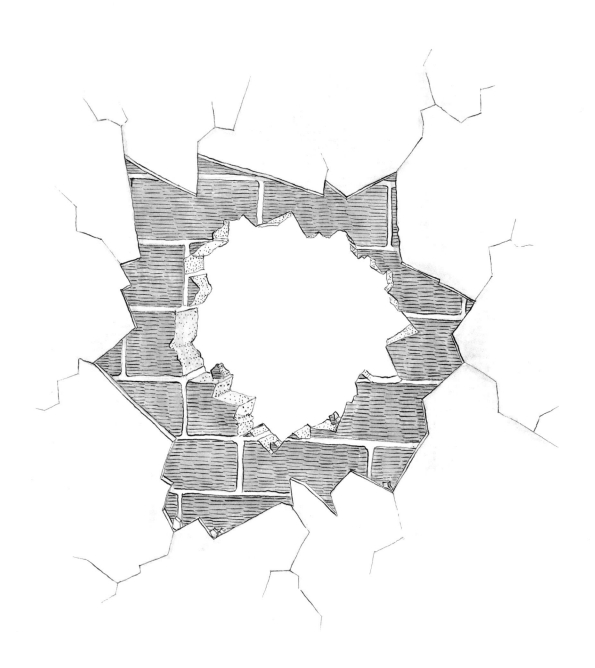

and finally come to rest . . .

. . . in Mrs. McBeaver's oatmeal.

Eugene would have been in very big trouble.

He might have had to leave home

and join the circus,

or stow away on a ship
bound for South America . . .

. . . to live with an isolated tribe in the Amazon

where nobody would know his past.

Or he might have had to become a hermit on a Himalayan mountain,

drinking cups of tea.

He might have had to become a monk . . .

. . . in a monastery on a Greek island,

and never speak another word.

He might have fallen in with bad company,

and spent his life on the run.

But Eugene ended up . . .

. . . going home for lunch,

because . . .

. . . Karl caught the ball!

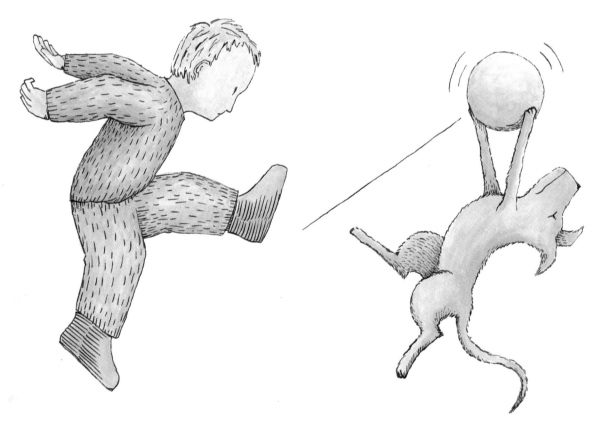